STERLING CHILDREN'S BOOKS
New York

An Imprint of Sterling Publishing
387 Park Avenue South
New York, NY 10016

ISBN 978-1-4027-8343-2

Distributed in Canada by Sterling Publishing
c/o Canadian Manda Group, 165 Dufferin Street
Toronto, Ontario, Canada M6K 3H6
Distributed in the United Kingdom by GMC Distribution Services
Castle Place, 166 High Street, Lewes, East Sussex, England BN7 1XU
Distributed in Australia by Capricorn Link (Australia) Pty. Ltd.
·   P.O. Box 704, Windsor, NSW 2756, Australia

For information about custom editions, special sales, and
premium and corporate purchases, please contact Sterling Special Sales
at 800-805-5489 or specialsales@sterlingpublishing.com.

Manufactured in China
Lot #:
2   4   6   8   10   9   7   5   3   1
08/14

www.sterlingpublishing.com/kids

SILVER PENNY STORIES

Beauty and the Beast

Told by Kathleen Olmstead
Illustrated by Linda Olafsdottir

Once upon a time, there was a kindhearted girl named Beauty. She lived in the woods with her father and her two sisters.

Beauty woke up early every morning. She cleaned the house and cooked all the meals. Beauty loved helping her father. Beauty also liked to read books. She was very happy.

One day, Beauty's father, Mr. Beaumont, went on a trip. Beauty's sisters asked him to bring them pretty dresses and fancy presents. Beauty asked for a rose. "Something simple and beautiful," she said.

Coming home, Mr. Beaumont lost his way in a storm. He was frightened and cold. Then he saw a castle in the woods.

Mr. Beaumont went inside. No one was home, but he found a warm dinner, a fire, and a bed. In the morning, dry clothes were waiting for him.

As Mr. Beaumont was leaving, he saw a rosebush. He picked a flower for Beauty. Suddenly he heard a loud, terrible growl. "How dare you!"

A beast appeared beside him.

"You repay kindness by stealing from me?" Beast growled.

Mr. Beaumont explained that the rose was for his daughter.

"Then your daughter must pay. Bring her to me," Beast said.

At home, Mr. Beaumont's daughters listened to his story.

"I will not let him take you," he said to Beauty.

She shook her head. "No. I will go, Father."

Beauty went to Beast's castle.

It was very scary, but Beauty tried

to be brave.

"I want you to be comfortable,"

Beast said.

This made Beauty feel better.
She was surprised that he was kind.

"I wish I could see my father again," she said.

Beast gave Beauty a magic mirror. She could see her father in the mirror whenever she wanted. Beauty did not feel so far from home anymore.

Beast filled Beauty's room with
books and a piano. Every evening,
she ate a delicious dinner. One night
Beast said, "Beauty, I love you.
Will you marry me?"

Beauty thought Beast was kind,
but she did not love him. "I'm sorry,"
she said. "I cannot marry you, but
I will be your friend."

Beauty looked into her mirror.
Her father was very sick. "I must
go home!" she cried.

Beast said, "Of course. Please
return soon, though. I will be lost
without you."

Using Beast's magic, Beauty was home in an instant. Her father was very happy to see her. Soon, he was all better.

Beauty was happy to be home, but she missed Beast. "I am lost without him," she said.

Beauty rushed back to the castle.

Beauty found Beast. "I love you!"
she said.

As soon as she said those words,
a bright light flashed. Beast changed
into a handsome prince.

"Beauty, will you marry me?"
he asked.

Beauty smiled and took his hand.
"Of course, I will," she said.

They were married in the castle,
where they lived happily
ever after.

He stood up. "A curse was put on me because I was too proud," the prince said. "I was turned into a beast. To remove the curse, someone had to love me for my kind heart."